FORBIDDEN WHISPERS

Summer L. Wilson

CONTENT WARNING

This collection of poetry contains explicit sexual content, references to sexual assault, and themes related to trauma, abuse, and mental health issues. Reader discretion is advised. This material is intended for mature audiences.

Poetry can be a powerful medium for processing trauma and expressing deeply personal experiences. The author's intention is to share authentic emotional journeys, not to glorify or romanticize harmful behaviors or experiences.

Take care of yourself while reading. It's okay to put the book down if certain content becomes too difficult.

Resources for Support

If you or someone you know has experienced sexual assault or abuse, please consider reaching out to one of these resources:

National Sexual Assault Hotline
1-800-656-HOPE (4673)
www.rainn.org
Available 24/7, confidential support

National Domestic Violence Hotline
1-800-799-SAFE (7233)
Text START to 88788
www.thehotline.org
Available 24/7, confidential support

Crisis Text Line
Text HOME to 741741
www.crisistextline.org
Available 24/7, confidential support by text

International Association for Suicide Prevention
www.iasp.info/resources/Crisis_Centres/
Resource for finding crisis centers worldwide

For those who set me upon my path as a writer.

To those who encouraged and inspired me.

Even to those who discouraged my journey. All of it led me to overcome my greatest challenges.

For my mentor of nearly ten years that helped me heal enough to publish my work.

To my creative writing teacher who reminded us that some of the greatest writers won't be published—not for lack of talent, but for lack of ambition and courage.

For writers who doubt their talent: may you find courage.

For those who have lost touch with love: may you rekindle it.

For those seeking to understand love: may you find clarity.

For those without a voice: may you be heard.

A Sacred Corner of My Heart

There's a place where love is held

For ones I couldn't keep near

A sacred corner of my heart

Where I'll love you forever

Even though we're apart

A Thousand Goodbyes

Under the guise of the good guy

You robbed me of the most valuable commodity

Time

I can't get those wasted years back

An honorable man would have let me go

Freedom

You took what you wanted with pleasure

I rarely received what I deserved

Love

Commitment

A family

I gave you a thousand beautiful goodbyes

I had to let you go, so I can finally receive what is
rightfully mine

And I lived

Happily ever after

Autumn's Sorrow

I told you could stay if you wanted
But I found you lifeless
and still that sad day
You weren't strong enough
to weather the storm
Sitting here
Writing this
I mourn
Tears fall from my eyes
when I'm all alone
An unfortunate event
You didn't exist, I was told
I would've given you a home
You were so small,
I could have been your mom
It would have brought me great joy to love you
play with you
and all of your toys
I act as though I'm fine
Maybe someday I'll meet you in another lifetime
So as I fall to my knees and cry
How could I lose you?
Why?

Beautiful Parts of Me

I only want to show you the beautiful parts of me
When I look in the mirror I see beautiful
When I take pictures from accentuating angles I see
beautiful
When I send you pictures of me I want you to see what
I see.
Beautiful
There was a time when I didn't see beautiful
but everyone else did
They saw beautiful
I came to love that girl
When she didn't love herself
That girl wouldn't leave the house without her face
done
Today, she does
Make-up isn't what makes you beautiful
How you feel about life, yourself, and the people
around you
Is what makes you beautiful
I've come to believe that beautiful is more of a feeling
rather than a look
Lighting up a room
The bounce in your step
That happy smile upon your face
The kindness you give to others
The love inside of your heart

That's what makes you beautiful

Better off Without You

While you were too busy to help me
I learned I could do it myself
While you flaked out on every chance
to show me you were my friend
that I was worth the time
I started to realize I was better off without you
When I asked you for love
you gave me sex
All of a sudden
I didn't need sex anymore
I gave you the love that I deserved
only to realize I needed it for myself
I fought
I fought because I loved you
I wanted to keep you in my life
I showed you what needed to change
but you never picked up those changes
You didn't evolve
And now, I must move on without you

Cactus Blossom

I love breathing in the smell of the desert air
The sweet perfume is beautiful and intoxicating
Enveloping all parts of me
I pause for a moment
when the scent tickles my nose
I breathe in and let it take me
It brings me peace
It means safety and spirituality to me
It brings me joy, like jasmine, too
Unique pleasant and fresh

Nothing compares to the beautiful desert air

Cardboard Box

You picked up my heart from the lost and found box
Seemingly, somehow, no one else wanted to find
But, you let your heart be mine, for awhile

For a season, we were together
Like a two for one drink special
Warming up the winter months
From beneath the flannel sheets

As springtime drew near,
I knew you'd disappear
Back to work and bust your ass
I'd usually miss you
This time, I won't wait
For your return and another half done, half baked date

Needless to say,
While you were away
After that last toss,
Back into the lost and found box,
I met another.
We didn't put it on the streets

Enigma

I met Vanora through mutual friends.
She had beautiful long smokey pink hair and tattoos in
hidden places.
Dark, heavy eyeshadow
Red lipstick and nail polish to match.
We flirted as she sipped on her macchiato
I loved staring at her cleavage bursting from her lacy,
black halter dress
I almost caught myself drooling
She exuded an energy that was hard for me to handle
We talked of deep subjects most women never talk
about
Then, she leaned into me and whispered five magical
words into my ear,
"Let's get out of here."
I took her to the bookstore I owned
I pressed her up against the glass door grabbed her ass
underneath her dress and whispered, "Pick out any
book in the store and it's yours."
I pressed my lips against hers.
I felt around her hips to unlock the door.
She was a kid in a candy store.
"I love the smell of books!" she said.
She indecisively bounced around from shelf to shelf.
Finally, she stopped at the sexuality section and pulled
out a book.
She hid it behind her back as she slinked towards me
behind the counter.
She bit her pouty lips.
The book was placed in front of me.
My eyes widened.
"The Kama Sutra. Huh," I said.
"What will be your currency for this book?"
"What do you want?" she asked.

I leaned over the counter and motioned for her to come closer.
"I'd like to feel you from the inside," I said.
She leaned back and asked,
"What do you mean?"
I spun the book around and pushed the book toward her.
"In other words, Vanora, I want to try out some of these positions on you. Pick some," I said.
"Oh god, I thought you'd never ask," she said.
With that, she picked up the book, threw it over her shoulder,
and climbed the counter.
Next, she was almost climbing me, ripping each article of clothing from my body and casting it aside.
She almost took my pants off.
"We should be more towards the back of the store, so we don't have an audience," I said.
We had a rhythm and were in sync with each other.
I picked her up from the counter, straddled her across me and waltzed her towards the break room.
We French kissed and made out with heat of a thousand suns.
She nibbled my lower lip.
I bumped a picture on the wall.
It fell to the floor.
"Fuck it," I said
I lowered her onto the table.
I untied her dress and pulled it down.
She motioned to take off her shoes.
I said, "Keep them on."
I kissed her ankles.
Her knees.
Her thighs.
Her hips.
Stomach.
Her collar bone.

Her neck.
Her jaw.
Lips.
I caressed her breasts and
sucked on her nipples.
Flicked them with my tongue.
I licked her down to her stomach.
I opened up her lips and exposed her pink, bubble gum
clit.
I put my fingers inside and massaged her clit with my
tongue.
I tasted her sweet cunt.
She let out a soft moan.
I loved her eyes, as she kept them on me.
Her scent drove me insane.
I couldn't take it any longer.
I wanted her on my dick.
I unzipped my pants.
I grabbed her ass and pulled her onto me.
With each thrust, she brought me closer to ecstasy.
I kept hitting it
Harder
And
Harder.
She was moaning louder.
I lost sight of where I began and she ended.
She said, "I'm about to come."
I kept going.
I didn't change a thing.
Same pace.
Same pressure and rhythm.
She kept moaning and then all of a sudden,
she was quiet.
I felt her closing in on me
So, I let go.
Her body pulsated and shook uncontrollably.
I pulled out and came all over her pretty stomach.

She was all giggles and smiles.
And to be honest, so was I.
I whispered sweet nothings and gently stroked her skin.
We got dressed and cleaned up.
As I locked the front door of the bookstore,
I asked, "When can I see you again?"
She thumbed through her new book and said,
"When you learn some more moves."
She giggled, kissed me, and pushed me away.
I drove to her car at the coffee shop.
The sunrise was beautiful on the horizon.
Everything looked more colorful.
She had an effect on me.
I kissed her goodbye and hoped she wasn't just an enigma.

Fall from Heaven

(Lyrics for the year of Corona)

Teardrops fall from heaven
Angels are weeping for all of humanity
How in the world can they save us
If we turn and look the other way?

There's a girl on the streets with her baby
Crying, "Please, come and save me.
I have no money, nothing to eat.
There are holes in the shoes that carry my feet.
I sit on the curb with my head in my hands.
Why can't you understand that you could be where I am?"

Teardrops fall from heaven
Angels are weeping for all of humanity
How in the world can they save us
If we turn and look the other way?

George pleading for his life.
Saying "Officer, please! I can't breathe."
All of this, from police brutality
There needs to be some sort of solution
We are not truly free.
So, we lower our heads put them in our hands
"Why can't you understand, that you could be where I am?"

We've lost so many, the death toll climbs.
What will it take for you to open your eyes?
Stop turning your cheek.
That's not what it means.

Everyone is so afraid to lose their lives
But what about the ones that have died before and for us?
Where is our hero now?
Is it the President? Our government?
A scientist in a lab reeling out new vaccines?
Protestors picketing day and night?
Fighting for things that should already be right
Essential workers tirelessly filling incessant needs?

What difference have you made?
When will you stand up?

How in the world can we save each other
If we turn and look the other way?

Falling

You
Are
Standing
On a plateau

Feel
The warmth
Of the sun on your face

Now, Run.
To the edge
Eyes closed
Arms wide open

Jump

Falling off of the edge
Is the very moment your eyes meet his
Getting lost in it's depths,
not caring to ever find your way out

Falling
Is the resounding beat of your heart
when you can sense he is near
Mesmerized by his intoxicating scent

Falling into pieces, melting
Whenever his soft lips touch yours
His taste is like poison, but none do you care
Rather you die for one last kiss, than to live an
eternity

Not falling

Fantasy

I know this familiar face
I know his staggered walk
I know not of why this feeling exists
Or even why I long for his sweet kiss

Through my veins, this passion flows
In which it beats my heart so
I long to hear his soft, strong voice
And what it has to say

While he would speak and I listen,
I'd watch his mouth
And this fantasy would begin to play
In my mind, even in the midst of day

Turn me around
Pull me closer against your body
Gaze deeply into my eyes and see my soul
Run your hands through my hair
Make my knees weak
My voice, unable to speak

Kiss me again and make me cry
For it has been too long that we've been shy
Slowly and gently unbutton my shirt,
remove this heavy armor from off of my chest
Caress my skin as I unbuckle your belt and drop it to
the floor

Kiss me once more but this time on my neck
I take off your shirt
My hands run down your chest
Lie me down
Undress me

Bareness
Nakedness
Time standing still
Kiss me all over and send chills down my spine
Take off your pants and throw them to the side

Once again look deeply into my eyes like a hunter
about to eat his prey
Whisper those sweet words I long to hear,
"I want you more than I can stand."
"You can have me. I'm yours tonight."
I want you to take me to the place, where I can see the
light.

I'm dizzy and shaking I can't see the ground
You brought me to this place I've never been before
Around the moon beyond the stars this moment of
heaven on earth.
Only silence is heard.
I will let you see this part of me inside vulnerable and
innocent
I swear our souls intertwined that time.
Trickles of sweat drop from your body onto my chest.
One more kiss to end this endeavor
Hold me tightly and stare into the sky
Two shooting stars just flew by
I can hear your heart beat as my head lies on your
chest.

I wish we could stay just like this, forever until the end
Two lovers hand in hand
I know it's time for you to go
I'll put on my shirt as you buckle up your pants
Pick up the blanket and one last kiss before I crawl
through the window
A flower you picked is held in my hand

* * *

Lay my head on the pillow and stare at the ceiling.
Begin to let go of this feeling, of this night and of this
life
Then in deep contemplation of when will I see him
again,
I realize how deeply I care for him
I love you. I love you my prince. I am your princess
you wake at night to come riding with you until the
morning sunlight

As I wake, the sun rises high.
In the mirror, I look at me.
I realize it was all a dream of fantasy.

Gold

You give of yourself a rose of gold
Given in which one does not earn
Until that love is given like my own
In the past I looked for perfection
Searching for what I knew wasn't true
Accepted by the defects that I hold
Where'd you put the key to your mystery?
So that I may unlock your heart
Love from Romeo and Juliet's story
From that of which our parents wouldn't allow
When I'm in your arms nothing seems to exist
Kissing your lips like no other soft kiss.

Imaginary Conversations

Imagine every conversation
With the same sensation
Of sitting on the very edge of your seat
Feeling the flutter of butterflies on your stomach
Your heart beats like a resounding drum
Ah, the wonderment of these conversations!
But he would only make a fool out of you
At the heart of these transactions, there are no words
Just silence, as you tango with these thoughts
That maybe, just someday, the two of you will take
each others hands
and walk down a beautiful path
Then the witch in your head said, "Dead, dead. It's all
in your head. Every last one of your muses dropped
dead."
But, you will not believe it, nor will you care
Sitting on the edge of your seat with the same
sensation
imagining every conversation
It was true
Every last muse in my head dropped dead
I became the muse, instead.

Love in the Time of Corona

Visits with you are few and far between, now
I try to savor every moment with you,
but it's never enough
I drink your body through my eyes
Memorize the outline of your face
I can try to deny it, but this is tough

Take my hand and kiss it
Kiss my lips and taste my tongue
I'm waiting for you to ask me to be your woman
Take me to the bed
Show me exactly where we stand

As we lie here in my bed, whisper,
"I love you more, then you'll ever understand."
Can we just stay like this forever?
I know you have to go,
but we'll always have the time we loved during Corona

Melt into me

The intensity of his presence shook me to the core

I looked him square in his grey eyes and said, "Kiss me
like you mean it. Last time I knew you wanted to kiss
me because I could smell mouthwash on your breath."

He shifted his stance and drew his face near mine

He pressed his lips against mine

The smoke from his Marlboros and the Jack on his
breath never smelled so good.

The taste of ecstasy from his lips never tasted so sweet

Tears welled up in my eyes.

I've waited for this for what seems like eternity

He removed every article of clothing from my body

And I removed his

Stealing kisses and biting lips

We tripped over into my bed

Recklessly, he tore through my skin with his lips and
teeth.

Ravished me as if he was starving and never had a bite
to eat

He grasped my hands and pressed them into the bed
above my head

The wind of his soul blew right through mine

He kissed and sucked my breast

My skin reddened and became flushed

We made love that could make angels cry

He melted into me like dripping candle wax lit from a
flame

I knew in this moment I would never be the same

Mile after Mile

(Lyrics)

There's no telling where the end of the road stops
Were meeting at a coffee shop
Been driving mile after mile
Me and my shadow singing along to the radio
Feeling fine. No wine and dine. Just conversation.

With a flick of an ash put on my rose colored glasses
Touch up my red lipstick, push open the door
Nervous exhilaration. Sit myself down
I tap my feet on the floor
The clock on the wall says it's getting late

Then he walks in with the breeze on this cold autumn night
Sending chills down my spine
Breathe him in deeply
Shouldn't I be sleeping?
Its nearly 3 o'clock

He's making these sly passes
Taking me back to his place

He loved me wrong
He loved me right
He loved me right til it was wrong

How can this be?
He doesn't love me
What about the moon and the stars in the sky?
What about our walk on the beach and that look in your
eyes?
Holding hands and gentle kisses?
Are we feeling blissful?

* * *

All I know is…
He loved me wrong
He loved me right
He loved me right til it was wrong

This is where the end of the road stops
We met at a coffee shop
Driving home mile after mile
Just me and my shadow singing along to the radio
Feeling fine. No wine and dine. "Just conversation."

Mistress

As I lie here upon the prickly grass
I gaze into the pure, untouched heavens
Wait here patient, look upon the hourglass
In this place, I hope we shall meet again

Is that you I see across the blue lake
Pain in my chest is felt like no other
Why my raving beauty, me, you forsake?
Aye me, tis you I see with mine brother

He spun you round, held you close, kissed your lips
Take this dagger pierce it through my sad chest
Run his bony fingers along your hips
Now lay me in the lake, forever rest

Passionate, poisonous, deadly mistress
Rather I be dead, then to witness this

Moonlit Love

I catch his glances as his eyes gaze over
my porcelain skin underneath the moonlit
sky.
He presses his lips against mine.
He runs his hands through my silky chestnut
colored hair.

He grazes the back of my neck with his
fingertips and unties my black swimsuit top
exposing my bare chest.

The waves crash in the distance on the
secluded beach.
He caresses my breasts gently and circle my
mocha colored nipples making them hard.
He licks my stomach and gropes my ass with
his hands.
He kisses my hips so deeply.
I can barely stand the sensation.
I yearn and crave him.

My hands travel down his stomach across his
sides and up his back.
He caresses my thighs.
I open up my legs after he slips off my red
bikini bottoms
He grasps my lady and my
juices flow onto his hands.
His eyes locked with mine he lowers his
head between my thighs.

He tickles my clit with his tongue
I feel the heat from his breath, taking in
big soft bites of me into his mouth.

He licks the rim of my honey pot, then puts
his tongue inside.
I grab hold of his hair and let out a
pleasurable moans.
He tastes the luscious honey I made just
for him.

I kiss his neck then grab his wrists and
playfully flip him on his backside.

I say, "I'm about to give you the ride of
your lifetime," and take off his bathing
suit and toss it aside.

I stand on the sand and straddle his naked
untouched body.
His eyes almost caress me as he looks me
over narrowing in on my lady.
He wants me.
I drop down low and get into the flow of
the motion.
I hear the sound of a sigh as I put his
erect, throbbing manhood inside the most
sacred part of me.
My heart races while we reach the edge of
ecstasy with each thrust of him inside of
me.
Each stroke of my body and him going
deeper, reaching the point of no return.
There's no going back from this point.
Hot, passionate, lip biting kisses.
Rapture fills both of us, as we lose sight
of everything around us.

Making love to him seemed timeless and
endless.
I let out a moan as we finally reach the

heavens of ecstasy.

Purple and deep blues permeate the sky.
I brought out the Angel in him.
He woke the devil in me.

Our souls intertwined for just a moment,
but a bond that lasts for all eternity.
We exhale in sweet satisfaction.
There's a glow radiating off of our
bodies.
Now, we're in a lovers embrace.
I trace my fingers down his back.
I playfully grab his manhood and giggle as
he pulls back from the sensitivity.
He looks me deep in the eyes as his body
hovers over mine.
We talk of good times and the future.

Hand in hand, we walk down to the water and
float as our bodies are tangled together,
swaying back and forth in the waves.
We watch as the sun begins to rise on the
horizon.

A new day.
A new love.
A new life.

Peaches and Cream

Our paths crossed and you fell into my world
You walk through my mind day and night
You sit on a golden throne in my heart
I yearn to kiss your soft, gentle lips
I want to run my hands through your dark hair
and gaze into your smokey colored eyes
You run through my dreams and fantasies of seduction
I hunger for the forbidden fruit in which you possess
I thirst for the luscious nectar from your flower
I want to feel that sinful, passionate heat between us
I would make love to you for hours on end
I would kiss every inch of your body
If you'd let me
My skin as soft as peaches
And cream sweeter than candy

Pivotal Moment

There comes a time in everyone's life

when they face a decision that

will change

the course of their lives.

Now, is that moment for me.

I'm not sure what I'm running from or to,

but I will get there.

Heaven is all around us.

Are we fighting a war that will never come?

Or is it something inside of ourselves?

I hope several victories reign across the world,

as we grow and become better versions of ourselves.

Relationships and Plants

Friendships and relationships are a lot
like plants, they say. Buddha was asked
what's the difference between like and
love?
"If you like a flower," he responded, "you
pick it. If you love a flower, you water it
daily." Plants need sun, soil, to be fed
and watered. People aren't too much
different. A little bit of time and
attention each day goes a long way. But if
you touch a flower, you could bruise the
petals. You bruised my petals, a lot. The
point I'm trying to make is that I needed
to be watered daily. You watered me too
little. And it's showing. I'm withering
away. My petals are falling and my roots
have out grown my pot. I showered you with
time, attention, love and affection. I
needed to feel grounded. I needed to feel
warmth. I needed intellectual conversations
that fed my mind and showered with the
right amount of love. I asked you for a
bigger pot, but you brought weeds. I asked
you and told you what I needed to keep our
friendship going. In caring for our
friendship, I watered too much. You put the
us in the shade, when we needed sunlight.
Finally, I've given up. I've always been
taught to care for my things, but I find it
better to care for the people in my life.
They mean so much more to me. You were one
of my favorite humans. I loved you, too.
The fact of the matter is, the grass is
greener where you water it and you didn't

water our lawn. I wanted us to grow in the very same garden right next to each other until the next season. Yes, I wanted more, but you didn't. And it shows, because our lawn died. So did our friendship. Although we were both wildflowers, I was more of a sunflower and you were more of a dandelion. I hope you find your wish, "your" dandelion.

Sacred

I crave something deep

I crave something sweet

I crave something powerful

Something...

Sacred

My body laid by your side

My flesh heated by the warm sunlight

My heart opened to you

I unfolded for you like a Lotus flower.

I became vulnerable for you

I was attracted to your strength

The divine masculine within

Something...

Sacred

We have an energetic tie

Something you can't splice

At the time we met, you met a different version of me

* * *

I was tangled and twisted

I came undone

I could barely speak at all, let alone speak from my heart

Yet, we still vibed

I knew we had so much work to do on ourselves,

but I knew it wasn't over

That's why I let you go

In hindsight, the choices we made were right

It lead me to security and freedom

A chance to start over

My whole world on fire, the town ablaze, as I walked away

I didn't want to leave you

I didn't even get a chance to say goodbye

I hope we reconnect

I hope you see beneath the lies and half-spoken truths

I hope you realize it was all sacred

The Art of Making Love

The playful game starts hours before the
endeavor begins
He interlocks his hands with hers
Every glance with a smile

A whisper of I love you lingers in the air
Running your fingers through her hair
Touching the edge of his skin

Oceans could not separate the lovers
Faded memories of a face she will never
forget

Music floats in the distance
As they dance along the boardwalk
Keeping in time with the beat, she sways
her hips
Instantly, he grabs her and twirls her
around
Never missing a step
Gently kissing her on the lips

Electric to the touch
A shiver sent down her back
Racing Hearts
The universe sparkling in their eyes
He bows and kisses her palms

Stars fill the night sky
He takes her to a secluded place
A passionate heat pulses through his veins
Tempting
Tantalizing
Every breath drinks in the aroma of his
scent

Ready to let go
Igniting her lust, he boosts her up on the
kitchen counter   revealing her
thighs underneath her white skirt
Next, she embraces him with her shivering
body, while he kisses   her neck
Grabbing her hips, he pulls her in closer
and presses himself against her lady

Trembling hands unbuckle his belt
A quivering lip caresses the inside of her
thigh
Now, she lifts his shirt above his head
The bareness of his stomach exposed
A warm hand travels up her back; He takes
of her bra with a snap
Leaving her breathless, she kisses his face
and bites his neck
Inside, he aches
Zipper pulled down, pants fall to the
floor, kicks them aside
Intertwined by her legs, he brings her to
the bed
Next, she gives him a gorgeous, come hither
type of stare
Gently pulling her hair and kissing her
breasts

Energies heightened
Love the way he kisses, she can hear it in
his breath
Enticing him with her tongue
"Can you tell I want you?" She asked
"Tell me you want me," he said
Ready to let go, yet hold on tightly for
this ride

Into the gates of heaven
Falling off the edge of reality
Young lovers climbing to a state of ecstasy
and bliss
Irresistible. He could never fathom a love
like this
Nothing compares to this flame lit in her
chest
'Give me all you've got," she commanded

"Let me get you there" he encouraged
Over and over again pleasure reached its
heights
Violets and blues permeate the room
Electricity brought them to life

"Tell me. Do you love me?," she whispered
"Oh, you know I do," he said

Moonlight illuminates the lovers' skin
Everlasting satisfaction seeping in

Unrequited Love

"I've come to the conclusion that I won't be letting anyone know how I feel about them first, ever again," she spewed. "I won't pine. I won't chase. I won't run. It kicks me in the ass and hurts me that I go out on this limb to let someone know how I feel about them and it only backfires into my face.
They either aren't in touch with themselves to know how they feel about me or it simply isn't returned.
It isn't my fault that I'm in touch with myself, that I know and express my feelings more readily than most. So, all the while you guys are jerking your dicks to get off on me; Until I find a wild enough spirit, my knight in shining tinfoil, to run along side of me on this crazy planet Earth, I will do what I want and play. I was never meant to be tamed!"

Up in smoke

As I smoked what I hope what would be my last cigarette
I had been vaping instead to feed my nicotine addiction
I could taste the familiarity of that first dirty, dull, stale puff of smoke.
And I thought to myself why on earth would anyone want to smoke these, like I had the first time I tried one?
It's not the taste or look cool or sexy.
It was to feed the addiction unto itself once it is triggered.
That's why I kept smoking.
The addiction.
But what was the reason behind smoking that I had truly started?
It was to have a sense of belonging to my peers.
Facebook addiction? Same. Food? Same. Well, sometimes. Drugs? Alcohol? Gambling? Sex?
Which is rooted in our need to feel loved, wanted and accepted. Are we forever chasing the first high we felt of being loved? We never became unlovable. We simply stopped remembering to be ourselves.

Weeping Willow

Weeping Willow, don't cry
Everything will be alright

The wind blows through its elegant leaves
On a cool moonlit night

A strange, uncomfortable silence
Is broken by her screams,
But her voice goes unheard

His boney cold hands run up her thighs

This demon from hell devours innocent souls
To give him a wicked kind of high

Pureness, bareness
Skin is all that remains

What will become of this tainted beauty?

Her life was shattered in an instant
Confusion filled her head

A spirited, vibrant soul turned cold, empty, and dark
The comfort of insanity will never leave her side
From the sunlight she hides

Her face is now worn and will never look the same as it
did before that horrible day
Tears pour down from her eyes at night, when
everything is not quite right

She keeps this secret locked up
It eats her soul inside

* * *

Years later, at the lake, she held a gun to her head.
Before she pulled the trigger this is what she said,

"Weeping willow hear my desperate cry- everything
will never be alright inside."

Everything once felt before, does not exist anymore.

What it is, what it isn't

I know what love is

I know what it isn't

Love is easy, but not without trials and tribulations

Love isn't manipulation, coercion, and exploitation

Romantic love can feel passionate

It doesn't shame

Love feels playful, wild, and free

It doesn't confine, abuse, or neglect

Love is an enthusiastic, "Yes!"

Love isn't shut down, silent, and frozen in time

Love can feel like a deep friendship

If it feels forced, let it go

Love is a warm feeling in your chest

Love isn't feeling scared or fearful

Love respects

It doesn't control

Love is consideration

* * *

It isn't selfish

Love protects

It doesn't hit

Love forgives and has boundaries

It doesn't use

Love will be met with conflict, triggers, and trauma

How we deal with it, is everything

Trauma, triggers, and conflict can be healed with self-love

Unravel, inspect, and heal

Love will shine a light on what needs to be healed

Love anyway

Those who are meant to stay, will

Meet anger with the strength of love

Watch it melt away, but know when to walk away

Love isn't a reward for good behavior

Love is acceptance, with a side of evolution

Who the fuck do you think you are?

It came to me when I had Covid and I was at my weakest moment fearing deeply of the possibility that I could very well die- All the things I had not done, completed, felt, or experienced. Most of all fearing leaving behind my son and not completing the tasks I felt destined to carry out. I wasted my time on things. Not that they didn't matter, but I let those things get in the way of my priorities.

I was standing in the shower with the water pouring over me absolutely melting down and it came to me. A thought whispered, "Who the fuck do you think you are?" You have an infinite power of creating the world around you. You have a deep powerful capability of healing the people around you at a distance and you are sitting here doubting that you aren't strong enough to heal yourself. You are the embodiment of the universe. You are here to help raise the consciousness of humanity and bring more peace to the world just by simply existing. Here you are doubting that you aren't going to make it. The point is, this applies to just about everyone. We are much more powerful and magical than we could ever imagine.

Who the fuck do YOU think you are?

Worry is a Kiss

It's just between you and me
A kiss that speaks in tongues
Rekindling the flame
Breathing in us two
Devouring every inch of you

Here's to you…
breaking
    down
        the door
Here's to you…
A
shattered
    bottle
      on
        the floor
Here's to you…
Girl
   I
     Never
       met
         before
Now, we'll see who's
Worry is a kiss
Following us
Around
Downtown

Its me, who's kissing him under the covers
It's me, he's calling on the phone
It's me, who's kissing his third eye

We have a history deeper than you'll ever know
You're wasting your time
Leave us be

Yours to Claim

(Lyrics)

Come pick me up like I'm baggage claim
I'm just an airplane ride away
Run the streets all night long
Get tangled up and then come undone

Don't silence your voice
You're meant to be heard
After all it's your life to live
I'd love to share what's been on my mind

It was peace to be in your presence
I regret the things I couldn't voice
Being next to you was sacred bliss

Clinging to a fence I couldn't climb
Crying for a reason I couldn't find
Kiss my third eye
Let me know it'll be alright

I'm here
I'm yours to claim
I'd swim an ocean
How about you?
Climb the tallest mountain
Just to see you

Come pick me up like I'm baggage claim
I'm just an airplane ride away
Run the streets all night long
Get tangled up and then come undone

There's no one to blame
After all this time
I hope you still feel the same

Pour into your happiness
Follow your bliss
Don't let love pass you by

* * *

Clinging to a fence I couldn't climb
Crying for a reason I couldn't find
Kiss my third eye
Let me know it'll be alright

Don't let fear rob you of joy
If I never hear from you again
At least I know I tried

I didn't let love pass me by
I didn't let love pass me by
I didn't let love pass me by

Made in the USA
Middletown, DE
08 November 2025

20247662R00031